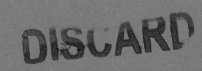

Abuelita (ah-BWEH-lee-tah): Grandma

hola (OH-la): hello

kimchi (KIM-chee): staple Korean side dish typically made of cabbage that is salted, seasoned, and fermented

Oppa (OH-pah): Older Brother (of a girl)

LEE & LOW BOOKS Inc., 95 Madison Avenue, New York, NY 10016
leeandlow.com
Book design by David and Susan Neuhaus/NeuStudio
Book production by The Kids at Our House
The text is set in Cotoris
The illustrations are rendered in watercolor

Manufactured in China by Toppan, November 2014
10 9 8 7 6 5 4 3 2 1
First Edition

Library of Congress Cataloging-in-Publication Data
Bahk, Jane.
Juna's jar / by Jane Bahk ; illustrated by Felicia Hoshino. — First edition.
pages cm
Summary: After her best friend, Hector, moves away, Juna's brother Minho tries to make her feel better by finding things to put in her special kimchi jar, and each night, whatever is in the jar takes her on a magical journey in search of Hector. Includes glossary.
ISBN 978-1-60060-853-7 (hardcover : alk. paper)
[1. Imagination—Fiction. 2. Glass containers—Fiction. 3. Brothers and sisters—Fiction. 4. Friendship—Fiction. 5. Korean Americans—Fiction.] I. Hoshino, Felicia, illustrator. II. Title.
PZ7.B14225Jun 2014
[E]—dc23   2014012484

JUNA'S JAR

by Jane Bahk

illustrated by Felicia Hoshino

Lee & Low Books Inc. New York

For Ena and Keo—J.B.

To feliyoshisorayume . . .
my family, my love,
my inspiration!—F.H.

Juna's family always had a large jar of kimchi in their fridge. After they finished eating all the kimchi, Juna sometimes got to keep the empty jar.

Juna loved to take the jar and go on adventures with
her best friend, Hector. They went to the park near their
apartment building to collect colorful rocks and small bugs.
Once Hector found a green caterpillar. Juna worried
that it wouldn't have what it needed to make a cocoon,
so they let it go.

One morning, Juna went looking for Hector to go on another kimchi-jar adventure. She ran downstairs to his grandmother's apartment.

"Hi, Abuelita!" Juna said to Hector's grandmother. "Can Hector come out to play?"

"*Hola*, Juna," Hector's grandmother said, giving her a hug. "I'm sorry. Hector is not here." Then she told Juna that his parents had come the day before and taken Hector to live with them in a big house far away. Hector had wanted to say good-bye, but Juna was not home.

Juna was very sad. When she got back home, her
big brother, Minho, tried to cheer her up. He took
Juna to Mr. Lee's pet shop and bought her a small fish.

Juna watched the fish swim in circles in her jar.

That night when everyone else was asleep, Juna put
on a diving mask and fins and dove into the water.

Juna's fish took her everywhere. They swam with sea turtles, played with dolphins, and discovered a giant clam.

"Can you help me find my friend Hector?" Juna asked her fish.

They swam to a dark, underwater cave. Hector wasn't there, but they found huge snakes slithering in the sand. When Juna got closer, she saw that they were actually tentacles. Juna wondered if they belonged to an octopus . . . or a giant squid.

I wish Hector was here, Juna thought. *He knows everything about animals.*

By the next day Juna's fish had grown so big its mouth nearly touched its tail.

"Oppa, my fish needs more space," Juna said to Minho. With his help, Juna put her fish in the aquarium in their living room.

Juna's jar was empty again.

Minho had an idea. He gave Juna a small bean plant he had grown at school for science class. They found some soil and carefully put the plant in the jar.

That night when everyone else was asleep, Juna put
on hiking boots and climbed down the plant into a lush,
green rain forest.

Juna swung on vines, climbed a tree with a sloth, and
sang with howler monkeys.

"Have you seen my friend Hector?" she asked them all.

One monkey pointed to the river and jumped away.

As Juna got closer to the water, she saw that the rocks in the river began to move. They weren't rocks at all! It was the back of an alligator . . . or a crocodile. She wasn't sure which one it was.

I wish Hector was here, she thought. *He would know.*

By the next day Juna's plant had almost reached the ceiling.

"Oppa, my plant grew too big for my jar," Juna said. Minho helped Juna put the plant into a large pot on their balcony.

Juna's jar was empty again.

Minho and Juna walked to the park. A cricket
chirped in the bushes.

Juna quietly snuck up to the cricket
and cupped her hands around it. Then
she placed it gently into her jar.

Minho helped her find twigs
and leaves, and they put them in
the jar too.

When they got home, Juna
punched holes in the lid of the
jar so the cricket could breathe.

That night when everyone else was asleep,
Juna put on goggles and a helmet and hopped
onto the cricket's back.

Juna and the cricket rode through the night sky together.
They flew over tall buildings that looked like giant steps
leading to the moon. They followed a trail of cars that lit up
the hill like a string of holiday lights.

Then the cricket landed on a windowsill of a big house. Juna peeked in the window.

There was Hector, asleep in his bed. And on the bedside table was the kimchi jar Juna had given him. Hector looked like he was having happy dreams.

Juna smiled. "Bye, Hector," she whispered. Then she hopped onto the cricket's back and flew home.

By the next day the cricket's antennae had poked through
the holes in the jar's lid.

"Oppa, the cricket grew too big for my jar too," Juna said.

So Minho and Juna walked to the park and set the cricket free.

Juna's jar was empty again.

Juna looked around the park and wondered
what she could put in her jar next.

I wish . . . , she thought.

"Look what I found!" a girl behind her said.
"Can we put it in your jar?"

Juna turned around. A green inchworm was wriggling
up the girl's arm. Juna smiled and held out her jar.